Published by Sweet Cherry Publishing Limited
Unit 36, Vulcan House,
Vulcan Road,
Leicester, LE5 3EF
United Kingdom

First published in the UK in 2020
2020 edition

2 4 6 8 10 9 7 5 3 1

ISBN: 978-1-78226-535-1

Text by Geronimo Stilton
Art Director: Iacopo Bruno
Graphic Designer: Laura Dal Maso / theWorldofDOT
Original cover illustration by Roberto Ronchi (graphics) and Christian Aliprandi (colour)
Internal illustrations by Claudio Cernusci and Maria De Filippo
Initial and final page illustrations by Roberto Ronchi and Ennio Bufi, MAD5 (design) and Studio
Parlapà and Andrea Cavallini (colour). Map illustrations by Andrea Da Rold and Andrea Cavallini
Cover layout and typography by Margot Reverdiau
Interior layout and typography by Rhiannon Izard
Graphics by: Merenguita Gingermouse, Zeppola Zap, Soia Topiunchi
© 2003-2017 Edizioni Piemme S.p.A., Palazzo Mondadori – Via Mondadori, 1 – 20090 Segrate
© 2020 UK edition, Sweet Cherry Publishing
International Rights © Atlantyca S.p.A. – via Leopardi 8, 20123 Milano, Italy
Translation © 2004 by Atlantyca S.p.A.

Original title: *Il tempio del rubino di fuoco*
Based on an original idea by Elisabetta Dami

www.geronimostilton.com/uk

# Geronimo Stilton

# THE TEMPLE OF THE FIRE RUBY

Sweet Cherry

# A MYSTERIOUS YELLOW ENVELOPE

Early one morning, I got up and ate breakfast. "Another day, another cheese Danish," I said to myself. Then I ran to the subway. I didn't want to be late for work.

Oops, I almost forgot to introduce myself. My name is Stilton, *Geronimo Stilton.* I run the most popular newspaper on Mouse Island. It's called The Rodent's Gazette.

Now wait, let's see, where was I? Oh, yes, I was on my way to the office. When I got there, I found a **MYSTERIOUS** yellow envelope on my desk. It was addressed to me. I recognised the handwriting. It belonged to Professor Paws von Volt.

The professor was a **famous scientist**. We became friends during one of my many adventures.

I slit open the envelope. My paws were *trembling* with excitement. Any message from the professor is always thrilling. But it wasn't a message that thrilled me this time. It was four plane tickets to Club Mouse in CROCODILIA.

Do you know where CROCODILIA is? It is on the Amazon River in Brazil!

Mr. Geronimo Stilton
Publisher, The Rodent's Gazette
17 Swiss Cheese Centre
New Mouse City, Mouse Island

The tickets were made out to me, my nephew Benjamin, my sister Thea and my cousin Trap. I wondered why the professor needed our help in the Amazon. It was all very **MYSTERIOUS**.

I called my sister. She is the special correspondent for The Rodent's Gazette.

"Hold on to your whiskers! I have incredible news!" I announced. "Professor von Volt has sent us tickets to join him in the Amazon!"

My sister squeaked so loud my ears rang. "**HOLEY CHEESE!** What a fabumouse scoop for The Rodent's Gazette!" she cried. "You get the gear. I'll tell the others. We'll meet at the airport in fifteen minutes."

One thing you should know about my sister: **she LOVES to give orders.**

# MY EARS ARE NOT STUFFED WITH CHEESE!

I ran right away to Rats Authority, the best store in town for sporting goods. I picked up some stuff for our trip to the tropics. Then I **RUSHED** to the airport.

My little nephew Benjamin gave me a mouse-sized hug. "Uncle Geronimo, I'm so glad I'm going with you!" he squeaked.

I smiled. Oh, how I **love** that nephew of mine.

Just then, my sister started yelling.

"Did you get everything, **Gerry Berry**? Well? Well?" she demanded.

When I didn't answer right away, she pinched my tail.

10

"Are your ears stuffed with cheese, **Geronimoid**?" she added.

Did I mention my sister can be a **pain in my fur**?

Thea popped open my suitcase. Then she began digging through it. I had packed four pairs of waterproof knee-high boots, four pairs of comfy camouflage trousers, four hats with mosquito netting, a first-aid kit and more.

"Looks like you have everything," Thea said approvingly.

But right then, a voice chimed in. "Everything? Are you kidding?" it scoffed. "If it weren't for me you would have forgotten the most important thing – **FOOD!**"

I turned around, but I knew already who was squeaking. It was my cousin Trap. That mouse could eat a five-hundred-pound rodent under the table. Yes, eating was not just a hobby for Trap. **It was his life!**

Now he waved a piece of Swiss cheese under my snout. "Go ahead, try it, **Cousinkins**," he ordered. But before I could open my mouth, he swallowed it in one gulp.

# I WAS FURIOUS.

"Ha-ha-ha! You always fall for it, **Germeister**!" Trap guffawed.

Then he showed me a little silver knife he wore around his neck. "I just finished a cheese-tasting course," he explained. "I always wear this little knife around my neck. You never know when something yummy may pass your way."

Suddenly, a **BIG, BEEFY** rodent in a muscle T-shirt walked by. He was munching on a Cheddar sandwich. Trap took one look at that sandwich and whipped out his knife. Before I could stop him, he'd sliced off a piece of it!

Muscle Mouse turned around. He was **INFURIATED**. And he was glaring right at me. "Hey, you! What do you think you're doing?" he shrieked.

I tried to explain, but he wouldn't listen.

"If I catch you, I will tie your tail into knots!" he shouted, chasing after me.

I hid in the bathroom.

**CHEESE NIBLETS!** This trip was getting off to a **TERRIBLE** start!

# IF I CATCH YOU, I WILL REARRANGE YOUR FUR!

Five hours later, the plane was ready to take-off. I was still hiding in the bathroom. What else could I do? I didn't want to get mashed to a pulp by old Muscle Mouse. I could hear him squeaking outside.

"If I catch that rotten mouse, **I'll twist off his tail!** **I'll rearrange his fur!**" he growled.

My teeth were chattering so fast, they could have won a tap dancing contest. I waited until the last possible moment to leave the bathroom.

"Last call for Flight 285 departing for CROCODILIA! Last call!" a voice announced.

This was it. I had to make a break for it. Quiet as a mouse, I slipped out of the bathroom. Then I

15

**RACED** for the plane. Paws pounded after me. "Come back here, you no-good **CHEESE NIBBLER!**" I heard Muscle Mouse screech.

With one last gasp, I jumped onboard the plane. A few minutes later, we took off.

The trip was very long. After all, the Amazon River is not on Mouse Island. It is far, far away in South America. **That's a whole other continent!**

# Big-Time Fun!

Finally, we arrived. A tall, lanky mouse with red shorts, curly fur and a purple ponytail greeted us.

"Welcome to Club Mouse!" he yelled. "Are you ready for some **big-time fun**? We've got **big-time** volleyball! We've got **big-time** water polo! You name it, we've got it – **big time**!" He was jumping up and down like an aerobics instructor.

I rolled my eyes. Oh, how I hate these types of resorts. I'm not into organised activities. I just like to do my own thing. I couldn't wait for the professor to show up.

Then I noticed Ponytail Mouse was staring at me. "You need to turn that pout inside out, Stilton. **Big time!**" he said.

Before I could stop him, he began *tickling* the bottom of my paws. I rolled on the ground in a fit of giggles. Can you guess why? I am **VERY TICKLISH!**

"Excellent! Now you've got it, Stilton!" Ponytail Mouse shrieked. Then he waved his tail in the air. "Theme song!" he called out.

Five sweaty mice appeared out of nowhere. They began to dance and sing.

"Here at the club, we're into big-time fun.
We like to swim and dance and sing,
we like to do most anything.
So join on in now, don't be shy,
give snorkelling a big-time try.
Yes, at Club Mouse we never frown,
and if you do, we'll track you down!"

When the song ended, Ponytail Mouse clapped his paws. "Hello, rodents and gentlemice!" he yelled. "I am the head of this club! My name is **ROWDYRAT**

18

**BIGTIME!** I'd like to remind you that our hee-hee ha-ha lessons start at six o'clock!"

Hee-hee ha-ha lessons? What were they? Probably some ridiculous Club Mouse ritual. I shook my head. Did I tell you I **HATE** organised activities? I glanced at my watch. It was exactly six o'clock on the snout.

Just then, Rowdyrat grabbed me by the tail. **SLIMY SWISS BALLS!** He was dragging me up to a big stage.

I turned pale. I hate dancing. I hate singing. But most of all, I hate making a fool of myself.

"Let me go, **please!**" I squeaked.

But Rowdyrat didn't listen. He forced me to dance. The crowd roared with laughter.

Then Rowdyrat tickled the bottom of my paws again. I rolled around in the sand in a fit of giggles. Oh, why did I have to be so ticklish?

"Stilton, you're going to have big-time fun even if it kills you!" Rowdyrat insisted.

I groaned ... **BIG TIME.**

Meanwhile, Rowdyrat was busy making more announcements. "I **love** you all, Club Mousers!" he yelled to the crowd. Everyone cheered. "And now it's time for our water polo tournament!" he continued. "Last one in the pool is a **ROTTEN RODENT**!"

The crowd made a mad dash for the water. I made a mad dash for my hotel room. I'd had enough of this big-time nonsense. Enough to last a lifetime! **I couldn't wait for Professor von Volt to arrive.**

# THESE ARE CALLED CLICK-CLICKS!

Ten minutes later, Benjamin skipped into my room. A **huge grin** spread across his face. "Uncle, look! I caught a crab," he squeaked happily.

He held out a disgusting orange crab that had a ferocious look.

My fur stood on end. "Wh-where did you find it?" I stammered.

Benjamin pointed outside. "Right there, on the beach. Rowdyrat Bigtime taught me how to fish for crabs," he explained. "He said these are called **click-clicks**. I don't know why, though."

I started to tell him to put the crab back when tragedy struck. First that **HIDEOUS** creature glared at me. Then it jumped at me and pinched my tail with its claws. **Click-click!**

# "OW! OW! OWWWWWWWWWWW!"

I shrieked at the top of my lungs.

"Uncle, are you OK?" Benjamin cried.

I didn't want to alarm my nephew. "Let me explain to you why they call it a **click-click**," I mumbled. **Then I fainted.**

# WHEN IN DOUBT, I GIVE AN INJECTION

I came to in the hospital. "What ... where am I ... the crab ... **click-click** ..." I babbled.

Dr. Wacky Whiskers held up a long, pointy needle. "When in doubt, I give an injection," he said. "Everything gets better with an injection."

My eyes nearly popped out of my fur. Quick as a flash, I jumped out of bed.

I raced for the door, screaming, "It's a miracle! **I'M CURED!**"

Oh, when was Professor von Volt going to get here?

I found Benjamin in my room. "Uncle, how do you feel?" he asked.

Just then, **ROWDYRAT** poked his snout in the door. He tried to tickle me. I bounced into the air ... and landed on a **SEA URCHIN**.

**"YOWEE!"** I shrieked.

"Uncle, I'm so sorry," my nephew apologised. "Rowdyrat helped me find that sea urchin on the beach."

I should have known. That obnoxious rodent was getting to be a **big-time** pain in my fur!

They carried me back to the hospital on a stretcher.

Dr. Wacky Whiskers shook his head. "You again, Stilton?" he mumbled. He grasped a syringe. "When in doubt, I give an injection. Everything gets better with an injection!" he declared.

This time, I didn't have the strength to run. **Oh, how did I get myself into such a mess?!**

# WORSE THAN TUTANKHAMEN'S MUMMY

Thea and Trap came to see me in the hospital.

"This place is great!" Thea squeaked.

"I'm enjoying myself **big time**. Today I took aerobics, windsurfing, waterskiing, kickboxing and deep-sea diving lessons!"

Trap nodded. "I'm having the **BEST** time, too!" he agreed. "I played **big-time** soccer with Rowdyrat. Then I stuffed myself **big time** at the Chuckle Cheese Hut."

"Sounds great," I mumbled. But I was lying. I'm not much of a sportsmouse. And who knows what kind of cheap food they serve at a place called the Chuckle Cheese Hut.

As soon as I felt better, I decided to go to the beach with Benjamin. I dipped my paw in the water. **Brrr!** It was cold. Maybe I'd stick to sunbathing.

Just then, a mouse came racing right for me. He was screaming something.

I groaned. It was **ROWDYRAT**. I dove into the water to get away from him. That's when I found myself in the middle of a school of jellyfish! They stung me all over – even on the tail! **RATS!**

Rowdyrat pulled me out of the water. "I was trying to warn you that there are **big-time** jellyfish in there," he said.

Dr. Wacky Whiskers shook his head when he saw me. "Stilton. What a surprise," he smirked.

He smeared a disgusting, stinky cream all over my fur. Then he wrapped me up in bandages. I was more preserved than TVTANKHAM€N'S MVMMY!

"When in doubt, I like to give an injection," the doctor told me. As if I didn't know that already! He pulled out his long needle.

I was horrified. I was queasy. I was never so glad to see my cousin Trap in all my life! He **WHISKED** me away in a wheelbarrow before old Wacky Whiskers could stick me again.

**Oh, I couldn't wait for Professor von Volt to arrive.**

# WOULD YOU PREFER WIND, STENCH OR MOSQUITOES?

The next morning, Benjamin and I went to the beach. I stretched out on the sand with my book, *Inspector Cheesy Cracks the Case*. I love reading silly mysteries when I'm on holiday.

Ah, now this was the life. The sun, the sand, the surf ... the wind?? Yes, the wind was so strong, it nearly ripped my whiskers off! **RATS!**

I packed up my things. We moved to another beach. Yes, this was more like it.

No wind on this beach. But what was that awful smell? I grabbed my nose. The stench was worse than my cousin Stinkyfur after a workout. **IT STANK!**

Once again, we moved to another beach. **CHEESE NIBLETS!** This one was infested with mosquitoes.

Oh, where was the professor? This place was a **NIGHTMARE**!

Benjamin tried to cheer me up. "Uncle, don't be upset. It's not so bad," he soothed. "What do you prefer – the wind, the **STENCH** or the mosquitoes?"

Before I could answer, a seagull began circling overhead. **SQUAWK! SQUAWK!**

I shuddered. I don't trust seagulls.

One time, a seagull stole my glasses right off my face. It took me ten hours to find my way back to my beach blanket.

GERONIMO       STILTON

Just then, the seagull dropped something on my head. It was a piece of paper wrapped around a heavy wrench.

**"HOLEY CHEESE!"** I squeaked. Benjamin read the note out loud:

Dear Friend,

I knew I could count on you. I will wait for you at midnight down by the river. Make sure nobody sees you. It is very important we keep our meeting a secret.

Mousey regards,

Professor Paws von Volt

I breathed a sigh of relief. **Finally, the professor had arrived!**

# LAND, SEA OR SKY?

At midnight, Thea, Trap, Benjamin and I went to the river. How would the professor get there? By land, by sea or by sky?

You see, the professor liked to use many different types of transportation: trucks, helicopters, submarines. They were all made in his laboratory. Every one ran on solar energy. He was always perfecting them. One day, the professor wanted to pass on his inventions to the world. A **planet without pollution** was his **BIGGEST** dream.

I paced up and down the riverbank. Benjamin stuck to my side like glue. "Tell me again, Uncle, about the time you saw the professor on **Mouse Everest**. That must have been so cool," he squeaked. "I wonder if I could be the professor's assistant while we're here. Can you ask him, Uncle? Can you? Can you?"

I nodded. The professor had never met Benjamin, but I knew he would love him. Who wouldn't love such a **sweet**, **adorable** mouse?

Suddenly, the water began FOAMING with waves. A yellow submarine decorated with cheese holes broke the surface.

With a loud **POP** the hatch opened. A pair of mouse ears stuck out.

"Professor von Volt!" I called.

"Stilton, *Geronimo Stilton!*" the professor answered. **"Welcome, my friend!"**

34

# THE IMPORTANCE OF BEING STILTON

The professor invited us inside his submarine, the *Vonderwater*. He explained how it ran on batteries.

"The top part of the sub is made up of silicon crystals," he said. "When the crystals are exposed to sunlight, the batteries are *INSTANTLY RECHARGED*!"

The professor led us into a huge living room. A Steinrat grand piano stood in the corner. I wished I could play. But I wasn't a very musical mouse. I had trouble playing the kazoo! Behind the piano was a bookcase filled with books. On the walls hung the professor's beloved collection of priceless paintings.

Besides the living room, there was a kitchen, an aquarium, a greenhouse for growing fruits and vegetables, and a computer room.

# THE **VONDERWATER,**
## PROFESSOR PAWS VON VOLT'S SUBMARINE

1. Silicon crystals that absord solar energy
2. Command room with turret
3. Periscope
4. Watertight door

5. Computer room
6. Machine room
7. Kitchen
8. Boiler room
9. Bathroom

10. Art collection
11. Library
12. Piano
13. Desalinisation equipment
14. Electrical centre
15. Underwater camera
16. Solar lamps

17. Planting beds
18. Aquarium
19. Motors and turbines
20. Screw propellers

"**HOLEY CHEESE!** This place has **EVERYTHING!**" I remarked.

The professor patted my shoulder with his paw. "Yes, everything, except a good friend," he said with a grin. "You are a true gentlemouse, Geronimo Stilton."

**I blushed**. But I noticed Trap rolling his eyes. He hates it when rodents talk sappy. "So, do you have anything to eat?" he asked, patting his tummy.

I groaned. Oh, why was I related to such an **OBNOXIOUS** mouse?

The professor offered us a plate of cheese sandwiches. Then he told us why he had brought us to the Amazon. "I am searching for an **ANCIENT** Incan temple," he began. "It is said to be hidden in the thick trees and plants next to the river. Inside the temple is a **giant ruby** it would be an amazing archaeological find. I thought you might like to join me."

We all agreed enthusiastically.

"Wait till they hear about this at school!" Benjamin squeaked. I told the professor how my nephew wanted to be his assistant.

Volt beamed. "That would be **FABUMOUSE**," he cried. "I really need a trusty rodent to take notes for me."

Benjamin was thrilled. **"Thanks, Professor, you won't be sorry!"** he exclaimed, giving me a hug.

# A Voyage on the Amazon River

Soon we were on our way. We sailed up the Amazon River. What an **UNBELIEVABLE** sight! The plants were lush and incredibly green. Multicoloured birds sat on the branches of the trees. Crocodiles floated like killer logs in the water. **ENORMOUSE** hairy spiders, carnivorous ants and poisonous snakes watched us from the shore. I shivered. I was glad I was on the sub. Don't get me wrong, I like wildlife as much as the next rodent. But this wildlife was a little *too* wild, if you know what I mean.

I chewed my whiskers to keep from shrieking with fear. I didn't want anyone to call me a scaredy-mouse. I forced myself to listen to the professor. He was giving Benjamin a history lesson.

"The first European rodent to land in the Americas was CHRISTOPHER COLUMOUSE in 1492. But he thought he had reached India. That's why he called the local people Indians. After Columouse, the conquistadors arrived from Spain. They were soldiers who conquered land in the name of the king of Spain.

"Next, adventurers from Portugal came. They colonised Brazil," he explained.

"Why is the river called the Amazon River?" Benjamin asked.

"Perhaps some of the soldiers saw native women sailing up the river, armed with bows and arrows. These **fighting women** made them think of the Amazon warriors in Greek mythology," the professor suggested.

Then the professor sighed deeply. He said he was worried about the Amazon rainforest.

Long ago, the conquistadors had destroyed lots of historic artifacts. They had forced the natives to give up their traditions. Today, greedy mice continue to damage the rainforest. They chop down trees and pollute the water.

"If it doesn't stop soon, we will have an

**ECOLOGICAL DISASTER** on our paws," the professor moaned, shaking his head sadly.

Along the river, we noticed huts made out of leaves. Native people armed with bows and arrows peeked out. When they saw the professor, they smiled and ran down to the river.

"These are the **Yanomami**. Like their ancestors, they live in the rainforest. The rainforest provides them with everything they need to survive," the professor explained. "They **love** nature and they respect it. We should all follow their example."

He docked the submarine. Then he embraced the **Yanomami**'s chief. **You could see that they were great friends!**

# THE YANOMAMI

We stayed with the **Yanomami** for a few days. We listened to stories around the fire. A **Yanomami** taught Benjamin how to make bracelets out of toucan feathers. Another painted designs on Thea's fur with sap from urucu berries. "I can't wait to show Timmy Tidytail at the salon," my sister gushed.

Yes, those **Yanomami** were fascinating rodents. I could write all about them in The Rodent's Gazette.

The chief explained how worried he was about the

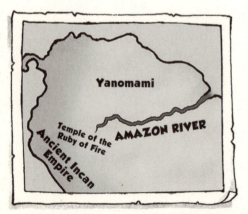

rainforest being cut down.

I nodded. Maybe I could write about that, too. "I will try to help you," I promised the chief.

Soon it was time to go. We said goodbye to our new friends. **Then we sailed up the river.**

## Yanomami

Today, around 32,000 **Yanomami** live in the Amazon. Their first sustained contact with western civilisation came in the 1940s and 50s. In the 1980s, gold was discovered in their land and it was invaded by miners. The miners polluted the rivers and destroyed the rainforest to build roads.

# A Mysterious Noise

Soon we reached the beginning of the Amazon River. We were in the land of the legendary **INCAN EMPIRE**!

The professor turned on the computer. He showed us a bird's-eye view of the rainforest.

"The plants are less dense here," he said, pointing to a spot. "I think that's where we should search for the **TEMPLE OF THE RUBY OF FIRE**."

We hid the submarine in a cove on the river. Then we trudged through the rainforest. We walked for hours, cutting through the vines with machetes.

I was **SWEATING**. My back was aching. And I had blisters all over my paws. **RATS!** I couldn't wait to get back home. I would book a whole day at the Restful Rodent. Have you ever been there? It's one of the most relaxing spas in New Mouse City.

Finally, we reached a tiny village.

The chief greeted us warmly. "Welcome, strangers. My name is Strongfur. This is my wife, Warmfur. And this is my daughter, Monkeyfur," he said. "Please, follow me, and I will introduce you to the rest of our village."

That night, we sat together around the fire. The chief and his family were warm and friendly. *I could get used to this place*, I decided. *It would be great to escape the rat race. Maybe I could even change my name. 'Brainyfur' might work. Or maybe 'Trustyfur'.*

I was still thinking about a good name for myself when the chief's wife asked, "What brings you all so far from home?"

"We are looking for the **TEMPLE OF THE RUBY OF FIRE**," Professor von Volt said.

Strongfur jumped to his paws. He had a strange look on his face. "There is no temple. There is no ruby," he said. "You **MUST** give up your search!"

The whole village repeated his words. "No temple! No ruby! No search!"

We were shocked. What were the villagers hiding?

Still, something told us not to argue. For once, even my obnoxious cousin kept his snout shut.

That night, I was snoring happily when a **mysterious** noise woke me up.

"What was that?" Thea whispered.

**It sounded like something buzzing.**

# WATCH OUT FOR THE BITERS!

The next morning, we asked the chief about the strange noise.

"Noise? What noise?" he answered.

"Noise? What noise?" the villagers repeated.

Deep in thought, I went to the river to get washed. I bumped into the chief's daughter, Monkeyfur.

"Watch out for the *BITERS*. There are a lot of them in the river," she advised.

I looked into the crystal blue water. I didn't see anything, so I bent over to wash my face. I wondered what she was talking about.

Suddenly, Monkeyfur began jumping up and down. "*BITERS*! Watch out! she squeaked.

She pointed to a school of fish headed for me. They were so small and colourful.

"Oh, those cute little fish won't hurt you. Here, fishy fishy!" I said, sticking my paw out. I grinned at Monkeyfur. She needed to get out more. Maybe I could help her overcome her fear of fish. Even a scaredy-mouse like myself had overcome my fear of the dark.

(Well, sort of. I still slept with my Cheeseball the Clown night light on. But don't tell anyone.)

Just then, I noticed something odd. The fish had opened their jaws. I saw two rows of teeth. Sharp teeth! **RANCID RAT HAIRS!** Now I knew what Biters were. They were **PIRANHAS!**

51

I jumped out of the river in three leaps.

Monkeyfur breathed a sigh of relief. My paws were shaking like furry leaves. I decided to rest under a tree.

But before I could sit down, Monkeyfur began screaming again. "Watch out for the **CAIMAN!**" she yelped.

I jumped up. **CLICK!** An enormouse crocodile snapped his jaws at me.

I headed back to the village. "Watch out for the tail that stings and the vine that strangles!" Monkeyfur called.

I looked all around. I saw nothing. Nothing at all. Was Monkeyfur pulling my tail?

"You are **looking**, but you are not **seeing**," Monkeyfur explained.

52

She pointed to a poisonous black scorpion hidden in the leaves. Then she showed me an anaconda slithering on a branch right over my head!

**CHEESE NIBLETS!**

Monkeyfur giggled. "If you want to survive in the rainforest, you need to use your eyes better," she advised.

I nodded. **"You saved my life. How can I thank you?"** I asked.

# 'C' LIKE IN CAIMAN

Monkeyfur showed me a notebook. "Do you know how to read?" she asked.

When I nodded, she looked impressed. It seemed no one in the village knew how to read or write. Can you imagine? Reading and writing are my **LIFE!**

"Only *they* can do it," Monkeyfur blurted out. Then she clamped a paw over her mouth.

"Who are *they*?" I asked. But she wasn't squeaking. I was dying to know what SECRET Monkeyfur was keeping, but I decided it wouldn't be right to pry. After all, she had just saved my life. Instead, I offered to teach her how to read and write.

We sat down by the riverbank. We began with the alphabet. "'**A**'like in apple, '**B**' like in banana," I recited.

Monkeyfur giggled. "I think I've got it," she said. Then

she pointed to a pair of yellow eyes watching us from the river. "'**C**' like in caiman," she said. She grabbed my paw and we raced back to the village.

Yes, Monkeyfur was a fast learner. **But I was the fastest runner with that croc on our tails!**

# IN THE DEAD OF NIGHT!

That night I went to sleep with my clothes on. I put my torch next to my sleeping bag. I wasn't taking any chances. What if a snake slithered under the door? What if a scorpion crawled through the window? What if my cousin put itching powder in my sleeping bag? Trap loves to play pranks on me. Once he tied a bell to my tail. When I took a step, I sounded just like a cheese-ice-cream van. Rodents came running from all over town!

I was sleeping soundly when I was woken up by a noise. It was the same **MYSTERIOUS** noise from the night before.

I woke Thea, Trap, Benjamin and Professor von Volt. Quiet as mice, we went to investigate.

We discovered a **HORRIFYING** scene. A

team of rodents was busy cutting down trees. They put the trees on a big truck. Soon there would be no trees left!

The professor was **furious**. "Scoundrels!" he whispered. "They have no respect for the rainforest!"

We decided we'd better keep quiet. I mean, these were rotten rodents. Rotten to the core.

One chubby mouse appeared to be the boss. The others called him Nastytail. His fur was slicked back on his head. He wore a huge gold medal around his neck. It said, **'I'M NASTY AND PROUD OF IT!'** He had a thick gold watch on his wrist. A glittering diamond hung from his ear.

"Bones, do this! Bones, do that!" he shrieked at a mouse as thin as string cheese. The mouse was wearing a black shirt

**NASTYTAIL**

decorated with skeleton heads. He had an evil expression on his snout. I shivered.

"OK, Boss, we're done here," he told Nastytail.

"Tomorrow night we'll change campsites. But we'd better watch out for those locals. We don't want them getting any funny ideas."

Just then, an **ENORMOUSE** rodent with a crew cut came strutting over. His paws were as big as my aunt Ratilda's ten-pound Cheddar logs. His teeth looked like they were made out of steel. His name was Mike Miceson.

**BONES**

"Don't worry, I'll handle them," he sneered, grinning at Nastytail. "If they get out of line, I'll just squash 'em!" He jumped up and down, punching the air. Then he punched a tree. It split in two. Part of the trunk fell on his foot. A big hairy spider crawled out of the trunk and bit his toe.

**"OWWWWWWWWW!"** the big mouse screamed.

Bones giggled under his whiskers.

Nastytail just rolled his eyes. "Miceson!" he squeaked. **"You may be big, but you have the brain of a bug!"**

**MIKE MICESON**

# THE STRANGERS ARE RIGHT!

The next morning, I talked to Strongfur. "We know about the evil rodents who are **DESTROYING** your rainforest," I said. "We want to help. We must stop them before it's too late."

Strongfur shook his head sadly. "I'm afraid no one can help," he said with a sigh. "They have threatened to burn down our homes."

Suddenly, Monkeyfur jumped to her paws. "The strangers are right!" she cried. "We must return to the **House of the Howling Spirits**, where the tombs of our ancestors are buried!"

"Howling Spirits?" muttered Thea.

61

"Tombs?" added Benjamin.

"OK, spill the beans," said Trap.

Slowly, Strongfur let us in on their secret. They were the last descendants of the Incas. For years, they had lived deep in the rainforest, next to the House of the Howling Spirits. It was the same as the place we called the **TEMPLE OF THE RUBY OF FIRE**. Then the **EVIL** rodents had come and began chopping down trees. Strongfur and the rest of the villagers were driven away.

I watched Monkeyfur listening to her father. She looked angry. "Father, please let me go with the strangers," she pleaded. "Together we will stop the evil ones. We should not have to live in fear."

After a few minutes, Strongfur nodded. He hugged his daughter. "You may go," he agreed. "But remember, **you must be sly like a monkey.**"

# THE HOUSE OF THE HOWLING SPIRITS

We decided to leave in the middle of the night. We crept on tippy-paws out of our hut. Monkeyfur met us on the path. She led us deep into the rainforest.

Even though it was night-time, it was hot. **TERRIBLY HOT**. Sweat dripped off my tail. And my whiskers. And my eyelashes. **CHEESE NIBLETS!** I felt like I was locked in the sauna at the Muscle Mouse. Have you ever been there? It's a popular health club in New Mouse City. I went in once just to check it out. I got my tail stuck in the treadmill. I dropped a pink dumbbell on my paw. Then I fell off the bicycle. How

**embarrassing!** Oh, well. You may have already guessed. I'm not very athletic.

I was getting to be a good observer, though. Monkeyfur had taught me how. I looked around. I saw all of the details I had never noticed before. I saw an **insect** hidden in a flower. I saw a **snake** underneath a mossy tree trunk. I saw a **caiman** sunk into the mud. I pulled Benjamin aside. I showed him all of these things. Now he, too, could learn the difference between looking and seeing.

In the meantime, Thea was busy **SNAPPING** pictures left and right. Trap tried to get in all of her shots.

64

"Cheese!" he squeaked, hanging from a vine.

All of a sudden, we heard another squeak. No, it wasn't really a squeak. It was more like a scream. "Wh-wh-wh-at is th-th-th-at?" I stammered.

Monkeyfur motioned for us to stay quiet. "That is the scream of the **howling spirits**. We must be close to their house," she whispered.

I gulped. I was scared silly. I mean, who wants to meet a bunch of spirits? Especially howling ones. I wondered what they were howling about. Maybe they were hungry. Maybe they were cold. Or maybe they wanted to scare us living rodents to death. Then they'd take over our bodies, move into our homes, and rearrange our furniture. **What a nightmare!**

**Oh, how I hate these scary adventures!**

TEMPLE OF
THE RUBY
OF FIRE

BULLDOZER

BOSS'S
HUT

CUT-DOWN
TREES

SLEEPING
QUARTERS

BATHROOM

TREE
TRUNKS

BOSS'S
OFFICE

TRUCK
PARKING
LOT

SUPPLY
SHED

SAWMILL

KITCHEN

WOOD SHED

TRUCK
LOADED
WITH
WOOD

TOOLSHED

INFIRMARY

FUEL
TANKS

# WHO DO I HAVE TO SQUASH, BOSS?

I pulled out my binoculars with shaky paws. I could see Nastytail's campsite. Then I saw something else. Hidden in the vegetation was a stone structure covered with vines. It was shaped like a pyramid. The only thing missing was a point at the top.

All around the structure were tall columns of stone. It was the remains of an ancient Incan village! Professor von Volt was so excited, he nearly **squeaked with joy**. Luckily, Trap put a paw over his mouth before he blew our cover.

"This is where our ancestors lived," Monkeyfur whispered. "We lived here, too, until the EVIL ones arrived."

We crept nearer. The shadows kept us well hidden. We listened as Nastytail barked out orders.

"Tomorrow, we will cut down *all* the trees surrounding the temple," he said. "Those trees are very valuable. Soon we will be rolling in cheese. But we need to speed up the work. I want it all gone by the **end of the day**!"

Bones chewed his whiskers. "Um, but what about Strongfur and the locals, Boss?" he asked. "What will they do?"

Nastytail let out an evil laugh. I guess they didn't call him Nastytail for nothing.

Miceson stood up and began punching the air. "I'll tell them what to do, Boss," he sniggered. "Just tell me who to squash and I'll **SQUASH 'EM**!"

He danced around in a circle like a boxing champion. Then he tripped over a log. He landed on a pile of red earth. It was a termite nest!

Miceson ran to the stream, **SCREAMING**. Bones was giggling under his whiskers.

Nastytail shook his head. **"Such a big fool."** He sighed.

# But Where Is the Ruby?

An hour later, Nastytail and his crew were sound asleep.

We headed for the **TEMPLE OF THE RUBY OF FIRE**.

Monkeyfur led the way inside. Flickering candles hanging on the walls cast eerie shadows all around. My heart was racing as fast as my uncle Cheesebelly at an All-U-Can-Eat Cheddar buffet.

Suddenly, we heard a **BLOODCURDLING SCREAM**.

"Do not worry. Those are just the **Howling Spirits**," Monkeyfur explained.

Just the Howling Spirits? I felt like I was about to **faint**. Oh, how I wished I were home in my safe, comfy mouse hole!

But before I could pass out, I saw something. No,

not just one something. A whole lot of somethings! A bunch of black monkeys were swinging from the beams above our heads. They were HOWLING at the top of their lungs.

Just then, they spotted Monkeyfur. They came down to greet her.

She spoke to them in a strange language. **"Ooo! Ooo! Eee! Eee!"** The monkeys answered her with a big group hug.

"See, they will not hurt you," Monkeyfur told us. "They are my friends."

Professor von Volt was busy studying the temple. He dictated some notes to his new assistant, Benjamin.

I looked around. In the main room there was a large, round well. A big, dusty stone covered the well.

"This is where I used to place the fruit for the **Howling Spirits** to eat," Monkeyfur said. "It was once a sacrificial altar."

Thea snapped away with her camera. The temple was **FASCINATING**. There were strange inscriptions on the walls in the hallway. And drawings of all types of animals and plants. I felt like I was back in the time of the Incas.

**"But where is the ruby?"** Trap asked Monkeyfur.

## Incas

The Incas lived in Peru from 1500 BC. Until the end of the fifteenth century, their empire included Ecuador, Peru, Bolivia, Chile and parts of Argentina.

In 1532, the Incan king Atahualpa was captured by the Spanish conquistador Francisco Pizarro, who took over the kingdom. The Spaniards destroyed the Incan treasures, which had immeasurable artistic and historic value. They melted the Incas' gold and burned their artefacts.

# A Column
## of Fire

Monkeyfur grinned. Then she pointed to the dusty stone covering the well.

## THE TEMPLE OF THE RUBY OF FIRE

**1.** Torches on the walls
**2.** Fresco
**3.** Sacrificial altar
**4.** Ruby covering the well
**5.** Well
**6.** Monkey-shaped tap
**7.** Empty terracotta jugs
**8.** Table where the fruit is placed for the monkeys
**9.** Entrance

Trap wiped some of the dust off the stone. Then Thea took one of the torches off the wall and held it over the stone.

"Well, I'll be a rodent's uncle!" Trap shouted. The stone sparkled in the light. We had found the **Ruby of Fire**!

"This stone hides a secret," Monkeyfur said. She told us the stone worked like a tap. When you turned it, precious drops of the **Oil of Fire** came out. The villagers had been using the oil to light their lamps for centuries.

I turned the ruby slowly. A few drops of dark liquid dripped out.

"Let me try that, **Germeister**," my cousin insisted. He pushed me aside. Then he yanked on the ruby full force.

"**Stop!**" everyone screamed.

**THIS IS HOW IT WORKS:** When you twist gently, a tiny bit at a time, the ruby makes the monkey-shaped tap produce a few drops of oil.

But it was too late. A huge spray of oil gushed out. A spark from Thea's torch made the oil burst into flames. The well became a column of **FIRE!**

We didn't know what to do. We couldn't exactly call **999**. But luckily, Monkeyfur came to our rescue. She slammed the big stone over the fire. **The flames died down all at once.**

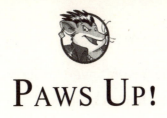

# Paws Up!

Just then, I heard a noise. **"Paws up!"** a voice squeaked.

We turned around. It was Nastytail and his crew. Fortunately, they had not seen the oil gushing out of the well.

"Hey, Boss. That's Strongfur's daughter," Bones told Nastytail. "Let's hold her **hostage**. That will make her father obey us!"

Nastytail nodded. "Good idea," he muttered. "I was just going to say that."

Miceson stared at us with a menacing look. "Who do you want me to **SQUASH**, Boss?" he sneered. "Just give me the word and I'll do it!"

Then he punched a stone slab. It broke in two and landed on his paw. A monkey bit his other paw.

**"Owwwwwwww!"** Miceson squeaked.

My cousin rolled his eyes. "What a bunch of nitwits,"

he scoffed. "You haven't even noticed the ruby."

Thea elbowed him to keep quiet.

But Bones perked up his ears. "Yes, legend has it that there's a **giant ruby** hidden here," he grinned. "We have to make them spill the beans, Boss."

Nastytail nodded. "Um, right. Spill the beans," he muttered. "I was just going to say that."

Miceson puffed up his chest. "Do what the boss said. Spill the bean sprouts or I will squash you!" he growled.

This time, he didn't hit anything. Instead, he twirled around in a circle, punching the air. After a while, he had to sit down. He looked dizzy.

Bones giggled. The rest of us kept quiet. The ruby was right under our snouts. But there was no way we were going to tell these **BOZOS**.

Bones thought for a moment. "Let's threaten to mousenap Monkeyfur," he said to Nastytail. "That will get them squeaking."

Nastytail nodded his head. "Yes, yes," he agreed. "I was just going to say that."

They grabbed Monkeyfur.

78

At that moment, the professor jumped up. "Leave her alone!" he commanded. "The ruby is here. Right under your snouts."

He pointed to the well.

The **ROTTEN RODENTS** stared at the glittering stone. Three pairs of eyes opened wide. Three jaws hit the ground. **"Jackpot!" they shrieked with glee.**

# OH! EEE! OOOOO!

The three scoundrels pounced on the stone like a hungry cat on a sleeping mouse.

"The ruby is **so big**!" Nastytail cried. "I wonder what it's worth."

Bones pulled a calculator out of his pocket. He punched in some numbers. Then he showed the total to Nastytail.

Nastytail gulped. "I'M RICH!" he shrieked.

Just at that moment, a few drops of oil dripped out of the tap.

Bones stared at the oil. "Boss, this is oil! There must be an oil well under this stone!" he giggled. "We won't be rich, we'll be **STINKING RICH**!"

Bones and Miceson slapped paws. "We're stinking rich! We're

stinking rich!" they chanted. They were so excited. They did cartwheels around the room. They looked like two mouselets on Christmas morning.

Nastytail frowned. "I am the boss!" he roared. "I will say who is rich around here!"

Then he ordered them to haul the stone away.

I noticed Monkeyfur waving to the monkeys. They had been watching us from the ceiling.

**"Ooo! Ooo! Eee! Eee!"** Monkeyfur yelled. In a flash, the monkeys sprang at the three villains. They began to hit them with stones and leftover avocados.

I watched with envy. Those monkeys were good shots. I wondered if they ever thought about starting a baseball team. But I didn't get a chance to ask.

Seconds later, Nastytail's two sidekicks had dropped the ruby. **"We give up! Make them stop!" the villains cried.**

# THE ARMY OF THE HOWLING SPIRITS

Monkeyfur shouted another order.

Immediately, the monkeys squatted in front of her. How **AMAZING!** They were as disciplined as a little army. She gave some fruit to the monkeys. They nibbled on it happily.

"For years, we have fed **the army of the Howling Spirits**," our friend explained. "They are the guardians of the ruby and our precious oil well. But we do not want to use too much oil. We should not waste what nature gives us."

The professor nodded. "Monkeyfur is right," he said. "Happiness comes from wanting only what you **need**. Too many rodents in the world today want **more than is necessary**. We are squeezing the earth as if it were a lemon. Soon there will be no natural resources left for future generations."

I thought about what the professor had said. He was right. We needed to **take care of our environment**. I vowed to use only recycled paper from then on. And maybe I could use less water. I could turn off the water when I brushed my teeth. And I could take a bath every other night instead of every night. Although that last one would be tough. I love a nice hot Cheddar bubble bath. It's a great way to escape from the rat race. **Cheddar bubbles, take me away!**

# THE TRUE GUARDIAN
## OF THE RUBY

I was still dreaming about that bubble bath when I heard a loud **CRASH**. I gasped. Nastytail had **SMASHED** the ruby with his machete!

"If I can't have it, no one can!" he sneered.

Monkeyfur burst into tears. "The ruby is lost forever!" she groaned. But for some reason a **strange** smile crept over her face. I wondered what secret she was hiding this time.

Trap tied up the villains with his rope. They sat glumly underneath a tall tree.

Then Monkeyfur led us to the other side of the temple. "I have a surprise for you!" she said with a wink. She pushed aside some banana leaves. They hid a narrow tunnel. At the bottom of the tunnel, I saw two yellow eyes shining. They belonged to an **enormouse**

boa constrictor. It was guarding a **sparkling ruby**.

"SSSSSSSSSS!" Monkeyfur hissed. The snake slid obediently toward her. I was impressed. Monkeyfur couldn't read or write, but she could speak two other languages – monkey and now snake!

The snake placed the ruby in Monkeyfur's paw. She explained that this was the real ruby. For many years, the EVIL rodents had been trying to steal it. So the villagers came up with a plan. They would put a fake ruby inside the temple. The boa constrictor guarded the real ruby day and night.

Thea turned on her two-way radio. She put in a call to the local police. "We have captured three **NASTY RODENTS**," she said. "They have been cutting down trees in the rainforest. Please come and get them. **Over and out!**"

# BE SLY LIKE
# A MONKEY!

The police arrived the next morning.

Trap led them to the tall tree. But the evil rodents were **gone**. Trap's rope lay on the ground in pieces.

My cousin blushed. "Oops," he mumbled. "I must have used my trick breakaway rope by accident. It's great for practical jokes, but not so good for catching criminals."

The police shook their heads. "Too bad," the shorter officer sighed. "We'll never find them. It's too easy to hide in this rainforest."

Just then, I noticed Monkeyfur giggling under her whiskers. "Don't be so sure of that. **Follow me!**" she said. I had a feeling that Monkeyfur was up to something. But what?

We walked along the path that led to the village.

That's when we spotted a deep hole covered with twigs. It was a trap. Down below, Nastytail was jumping up and down in anger. **"Get me out of here!"** he shrieked.

We burst out laughing. A little bit farther along the path, we saw Mike Miceson. He was dangling upside down from a vine. **"HELP!"** he cried. But what about Bones? Where was Bones?

Well, we came across him soon enough. He was trapped

in a wooden cage. Monkeyfur had caught every last one of them. She was **one clever mouse**! I was lucky to be learning from her.

"I was just following my father's advice," Monkeyfur explained. "**Be sly like a monkey**. After all, that is how I got my name!"

# The Headache Plant

The next day, Strongfur and the rest of the villagers, big and small, returned to their homes. They were happy to be back near the **Temple of the Ruby of Fire**. They invited us to stay for a while. I was excited. Now I would have time to finish teaching Monkeyfur how to read and write.

In return, she tried to teach me how to speak to the monkeys. I guess I wasn't very good, though. The monkeys laughed and laughed when I practised. Trap and Thea joined them. "Face it, **Gerry Berry**, you just can't squeak their language," my cousin smirked.

Finally, it was time to leave.

I started to pack my bags, but my head was pounding. I had a **terrible headache**. "I'm sorry, Geronimo. I seem to have lost the first aid kit," said the professor.

I sighed. Headaches are no fun.

I noticed Warmfur watching me. She stood up. "I can fix your head," she said. She ran away into the trees. Warmfur must have thought *she* was giving me a headache.

But she returned a few minutes later. She was carrying a little plant. The leaves were shaped like hearts. Warmfur ground up the leaves into a juice.

"Drink," she ordered, giving me the juice. So I did. I mean, I didn't want to insult her. But I was nervous. What if the juice made my tail **FALL OFF?** What if I sprouted **WINGS?** I closed my eyes. *Don't panic*, I told myself. It didn't work. I opened my eyes. I couldn't put my paw on it, but something was missing. I wiggled my tail. I waved my paws. Then I felt my head. Now I knew what was missing. **My headache was gone!**

Warmfur smiled. "This isn't magic," she said. "It is science. We call this the headache plant."

Soon the professor and Warmfur were chatting away about science and plants. **They were like two old friends.**

# I LOVE EVERY TREE.
# I LOVE EVERY FLOWER.

On the flight home, Benjamin snuggled next to me. He was filled with questions about the Amazon rainforest. He asked me about the animals who lived there. He asked me about the plants. I told him that many of the plants and animals in the rainforest are endangered. Pollution was slowly killing them off. We were losing some of the earth's most **amazing treasures**.

Benjamin shook his head sadly. "That is awful, Uncle," he said. He pulled out his notebook. Then he wrote **this poem about nature:**

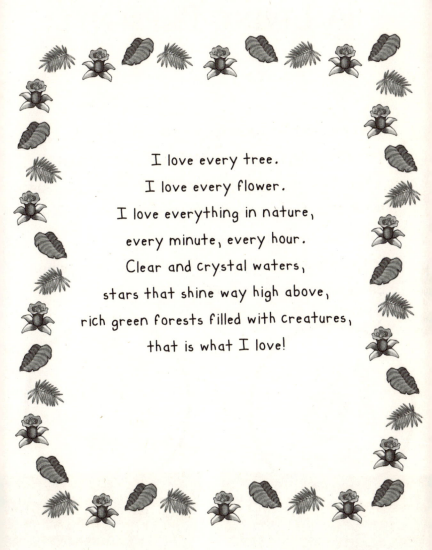

I love every tree.
I love every flower.
I love everything in nature,
every minute, every hour.
Clear and crystal waters,
stars that shine way high above,
rich green forests filled with creatures,
that is what I love!

# A LIVING PRESENT!

The next morning, I was happy to be back at work. Don't get me wrong, I loved the rainforest. But I missed The Rodent's Gazette. Plus, I wasn't crazy about sleeping in the rainforest. I missed my comfy cosy bed. And then there was my mega-huge fridge ...

I was thinking about my favourite cheeses when Benjamin burst into my office.

1. Take an avocado pit and stick four toothpicks in it about halfway

2. Fill a glass with water. Put the pit in the water so that half the pit is submerged and the other half is above the waterline. Change the water frequently.

"Look, Uncle! I brought you a surprise," he squeaked. "It's an avocado pit. You can grow it into a plant. I wanted to give you something **living**."

He put the glass on my desk. I gave him a hug. Isn't my nephew the **sweetest mouse in the world**?

Now he grabbed my paw. "Uncle, guess what? My teacher wants to know if you will come to our school. You could tell everyone about our adventures in the Amazon," he said. "Oh, can you, Uncle? Pretty please with a Cheddar ball on top?"

I grinned. **How could I say no to such an adorable rodent?**

3. When small roots have formed, plant the pit in a pot with good soil. Water it frequently so that the soil is always slightly damp.

# WHAT IS THE AMAZON RAINFOREST?

On Monday, I went to school with Benjamin. His friends asked lots of questions. I squeaked and squeaked until I was blue in the face. Well, I guess I didn't really turn blue. After all, have you ever seen a **blue mouse**?

## WHAT IS THE AMAZON?

It's a region around the Amazon River. It's huge: more than two million square miles. That's ten times the size of Texas!

It's covered with dense forest, called rainforest, because it rains a lot. The air is always very humid. It's hot; the temperature fluctuates between 25 and 35 degrees Celsius all year round.

## DO THE YANOMAMI REALLY LIVE IN THE AMAZON RAINFOREST?

Yes. They grow sweet potatoes and bananas, and gather mushrooms, berries and honey. They eat monkeys, tapirs and even insects. They hunt using bows and arrows. They also use blowpipes, which are hollow tubes that tiny arrows are blown through. Sometimes the arrows are dipped in a poison called curare. The **Yanomami** are good fisherman. They live in huts made out of leaves and sleep in braided hammocks.

## WHAT ANIMALS LIVE IN THE AMAZON RAINFOREST?

Some very strange animals like a bird-eating spider (8 inches long); the birdwing butterfly, the largest in the world (12-inch wingspan); and carnivorous ants, poisonous frogs and piranhas (fish that have razor-sharp teeth). Even the slowest animal in the world, the sloth, lives there.

## WHAT PLANTS GROW IN THE AMAZON RAINFOREST?

Strange plants grow there, like the giant rafflesia, whose flower is 3 feet wide and weighs 10 kilos. The pitcher plant is a carnivorous plant that eats insects.

Many species are even more mysterious, and scientists hope that these Amazon plants will help them to find remedies for some serious diseases.

### WHAT DOES THE AMAZON RAINFOREST RESEMBLE?

A building with many floors. The tallest trees form the canopy, up to 100 feet above the earth, where birds and monkeys live.

Underneath the canopy is the intermediate level, around 50 feet above the earth, where bats and snakes live. Below that is the ground, dark and humid, where jaguars, serpents and spiders live.

## WHO WILL SAVE THE AMAZON RAINFOREST?

The Amazon rainforest is a precious treasure for everyone in the world, and everyone must take the responsibility for saving it.

## WHY IS THE RAINFOREST IN DANGER?

Today, trees are cut down to create space for fields to be farmed and to harvest precious wood. Often, the trees are cut down illegally.

The destruction of the rainforest puts in danger all the species of plants and animals that live there. Many species run the risk of becoming extinct, which means they may disappear forever.

## WHY IS THE RAINFOREST IMPORTANT?

The Amazon's plants help to maintain the balance of the planet.

The earth is surrounded by atmosphere, formed by many gases, including oxygen, which is used for breathing. Even carbon dioxide is present in the atmosphere. If there is too much, the earth gets hot. This phenomenon is called the greenhouse effect, and it is dangerous.

Big forests absorb the carbon dioxide in the air and help to combat the greenhouse effect.

# ABOUT THE AUTHOR

Born in New Mouse City, Mouse Island, GERONIMO STILTON is Rattus Emeritus of Mousomorphic Literature and of Neo-Ratonic Comparative Philosophy. For the past twenty years, he has been running The Rodent's Gazette, New Mouse City's most widely read daily newspaper.

Stilton was awarded the Ratitzer Prize for his scoops on *The Curse of the Cheese Pyramid* and *The Search for Sunken Treasure*. He has also received the Andersen Prize

for Personality of the Year. His works have been published all over the globe.

In his spare time, Mr. Stilton collects antique cheese rinds and plays golf. But what he most enjoys is telling stories to his nephew Benjamin.

# THE RODENT'S GAZETTE

1. Main entrance
2. Printing presses (where everything is printed)
3. Accounts department
4. Editorial room (where editors,
   illustrators, and designers work)
5. Geronimo Stilton's office
6. Geronimo's botanical garden

# MAP OF NEW MOUSE CITY

1. Industrial Zone
2. Cheese Factories
3. Angorat International Airport
4. WRAT Radio and Television Station
5. Cheese Market
6. Fish Market
7. Town Hall
8. Snotnose Castle
9. The Seven Hills of Mouse Island
10. Mouse Central Station
11. Trade Centre
12. Movie Theatre
13. Gym
14. Catnegie Hall
15. Singing Stone Plaza
16. The Gouda Theatre
17. Grand Hotel
18. Mouse General Hospital
19. Botanical Gardens
20. Cheap Junk for Less (Trap's store)
21. Parking Lot
22. Mouseum of Modern Art
23. University and Library
24. The Daily Rat
25. The Rodent's Gazette
26. Trap's House
27. Fashion District
28. The Mouse House Restaurant
29. Environmental Protection Centre
30. Harbour Office
31. Mousidon Square Garden
32. Golf Course
33. Swimming Pool
34. Blushing Meadow Tennis Courts
35. Curlyfur Island Amusement Park
36. Geronimo's House
37. Historic District
38. Public Library
39. Shipyard
40. Thea's House
41. New Mouse Harbour
42. Luna Lighthouse
43. The Statue of Liberty
44. Hercule Poirat's Office
45. Petunia Pretty Paws's House
46. Grandfather William's House

# MAP OF MOUSE ISLAND

1. Big Ice Lake
2. Frozen Fur Peak
3. Slipperyslopes Glacier
4. Coldcreeps Peak
5. Ratzikistan
6. Transratania
7. Mount Vamp
8. Roastedrat Volcano
9. Brimstone Lake
10. Poopedcat Pass
11. Stinko Peak
12. Dark Forest
13. Vain Vampires Valley
14. Goosebumps Gorge
15. The Shadow Line Pass
16. Penny-Pincher Castle
17. Nature Reserve Park
18. Las Ratayas Marinas
19. Fossil Forest
20. Lake Lake
21. Lake Lakelake
22. Lake Lakelakelake
23. Cheddar Crag
24. Cannycat Castle
25. Valley of the Giant Sequoia
26. Cheddar Springs
27. Sulphurous Swamp
28. Old Reliable Geyser
29. Vole Vale
30. Ravingrat Ravine
31. Gnat Marshes
32. Munster Highlands
33. Mousehara Desert
34. Oasis of the Sweaty Camel
35. Cabbagehead Hill
36. Rattytrap Jungle
37. Rio Mosquito
38. Mousefort Beach
39. San Mouscisco
40. Swissville
41. Cheddarton
42. Mouseport
43. New Mouse City
44. Pirate Ship of Cats

# THE COLLECTION

## HAVE YOU READ ALL OF GERONIMO'S ADVENTURES?

# HAPPY READING!